THE VAMPIRE'S MILKMAID

JADE SWALLOW

Copyright © 2024 by Jade Swallow

All rights reserved.

No part of this book may be reproduced in any form or by any electronic or mechanical means, including information storage and retrieval systems, without written permission from the author, except for the use of brief quotations in a book review.

CONTENTS

Content Warnings	v
1. Anya	1
2. Xavier	10
3. Anya	20
4. Xavier	27
5. Anya	38
6. Xavier	51
7. Anya	62
8. Xavier	67
About the Author	73
Also by Jade Swallow	75

CONTENT WARNINGS

Please note that this is a work of erotica, not romance, that heavily focuses on breeding and milking fantasies. This book contains an age gap relationship between a human and a vampire and is intended for readers over 18.

A non-exhaustive list of content/triggers: Lactation kink (adult nursing fantasies) with the vampire hero 'milking' the heroine in the most filthy ways including use of fangs, breeding kink (unprotected sex), Daddy kink with the use of the words 'Daddy' and 'Babygirl', OWD (other woman drama/ love rival), instalove and insta-lust, size difference, fated mates, dirty talk, pregnancy including pregnant sex, oral sex, and typos and grammatical errors.

This is a work of fiction featuring imaginary scenarios. Do not try this at home. Only read if you are comfortable with the above themes. The author does not endorse the beliefs or actions of the characters.

CHAPTER 1
ANYA

When I got a job as a maid to a billionaire, I never imagined I'd be working for a vampire.

Clouds dominate the afternoon sky around the Tallon manor that stands on the cliff like a Gothic castle from the 18th century. Its spires rise into the morning mist, the cloudy gray contrasting the blackness of the building. It's like a scene from a horror movie, making me swallow with apprehension.

My tits are tight and achy. All that bouncing up the hill has made them even more tender and sore. I lightly rub them, telling myself I'll have a chance to milk once I'm at my new employer's house. After all, that's the reason I got a job as a wet nurse.

I press the bell and hear a deep voice that goes straight to my pussy. "Who is it?"

I recognize my new employer's voice which is rich as whisky and dark as smoke. I've heard it countless times on TV and on the radio. Xavier Tallon, the owner of the mansion is a multi-billionaire, who comes from a family of successful businessmen. With two Ivy League degrees, generational wealth that goes back ten generations, smoking good looks, and a self-created multibillion-dollar business, he's as close as you get to royalty in modern America.

My nipples tingle at the thought of meeting such a high-value man. I've never even seen a celebrity before, let alone a billionaire, but I know meeting men like Xavier is rare. At forty-five, he's still America's most eligible bachelor. With his pale skin, striking green eyes, and dark hair that's still jet black, he's got the kind of movie star looks I can only fantasize about.

"It's Anya, the new maid from the Hercules Agency." My heartbeats echo in silence as my employer takes his time to react. His voice cuts off, but the gates open with a beep.

I stare in awe as huge wrought iron gates capped with gold. I can hear the crowing of ravens in the distance. My sweaty palms clutch the steering wheel, moving over the smooth concrete driveway that winds like a ribbon. All around me are lush trees, and high bushes cutting off the view of the mansion from the sides.

I drive to the front door, trying to keep my head up. If the rumors are to be believed, Xavier disappeared from the public eye two months ago and hasn't been seen since. Nobody knows why he's gone; it's just that he's taking a break. The media speculates that he has a secret mistress and a love child. The fact that he requested a wet nurse makes me believe that he might have a child, but maybe I'm wrong. Either way, I'll never breathe a word about it to another soul. After all, it's part of the NDA I signed.

Though I'm not rich, I'm doing fine in life. After graduating from high school, I went through a bunch of odd jobs before I found my calling as a nanny and wet nurse. I didn't know so many people needed a lactating woman to help with their child. When I heard about how well the wet nurse jobs at Hercules paid, I knew it was my best bet to attain financial security at a young age. So, I used pills and massages to induce lactation and finally got my first job as a nanny and wet nurse at the most exclusive nanny agency used by the rich and famous. At first, it was just for the money, but as I watched the children I nourished grow happy and healthy, I began to love what I did.

It is incredibly fulfilling to provide such a service for my clients. Using my body to nourish children who need my milk makes me feel accomplished. A lot of times their mothers can't fulfill their needs, which is where I come in. Usually, I take care of the babies, and I'm paid really well for it. I love it when my clients appreciate my work. Maybe the inclination to nurture is part of my personality. I like knowing that I can contribute positively to someone else's life by doing what I love and what comes naturally to me.

Of course, there have been times when I've thought about having my own child to nurture. It's a little embarrassing, but I've been single for almost six years. It took me one date to figure out that men don't find lactating women incredibly attractive. To maintain my milk production, I have to eat nutritious food all the time, which has led to me developing curves. Though I'd never give up my job to get a boyfriend, I sometimes wonder what it'd feel like to be appreciated for my true nature.

I cut the engine, open the doors, and get off. The manor looks even more majestic up close. The agency said the house has been in the family for centuries, and Xavier is the current owner. Gathering my bag of supplies, I make my way to the front door. The exterior is made of limestone, giving off European vibes. Everything looks ancient, but it has been preserved really well. The windows are tinted with stained glass paintings. If I wanted privacy, I'd come to a place like this. It's so far away from civilization, that it's mildly scary.

I ring the bell, waiting with the ache behind my nipples building. I'm sure there's a child somewhere in this house who needs my cream. Most employers check the quality of my milk during our initial meeting, and if their child takes to it, they hire me. I'm expecting Xavier to do the same.

The door opens, and I paste a smile on my face, expecting to see a maid. But the man I see takes my breath away.

Xavier towers over me, six feet and three inches of pure muscle. In his black suit, he looks like a hero from a gothic novel, one who makes my heart beat faster. His electric green eyes, set prominently against his pale face, draw me in like a magnet. His hair is black and thick, cut short to finish his polished look. I spot a few strands of silver, but they're barely visible. My billionaire master has a straight nose and an aristocratic bearing. His charismatic form makes it impossible to ignore him. Now I know why the media can't get enough of this man. He's sexy as hell.

"Uh...hi, I'm Anya." I sound awkward. "From Hercules."

His green eyes roll over my body, surveying me and my bag darkly. My titties like being examined by my new employer way too much, because they begin to leak. I hope my padded nursing bra is going to do its job and keep my milk from staining my clothes.

"Yes, I have been expecting you. Come in." Xavier opens the door wider, letting me in. With my short, curvy build, I barely reach his shoulder. However, as I move past him, my fingers brushing his, I feel a chill. His hand is cold as ice.

Xavier locks the door behind me, ushering me forward. When I raise my eyes, I'm awed. It looks like I've gone back in time. The Tallon mansion is a majestic structure with a large, curving staircase in the middle of the house that reminds me of old movies. The checkered floor, the wood-paneled walls, the gothic-looking lamps, and the large chandelier hanging over my head, all add to the mysterious appeal of the place. The hallway is dark, the stained glass windows half-covered with curtains, barely letting in any light. Still, it looks so romantic.

"Wow, this place is beautiful." The words escape my mouth.

Xavier turns to me with a nod. "Thank you. This manor has been in my family for generations. It's one of my favorite places to be." His smoky voice makes me forget where I am, weaving a hypnotic spell on my body. Everything about this place is like a gothic story. "If you get hired, you'll be living here."

I swallow, realizing I'm here for a job. But the thought of living in this huge house with Xavier gets my pussy excited. It doesn't take a lot to figure out that I'm incredibly attracted to this man. There's something sturdy and dependable about him, and that's what a girl like me needs.

"Umm...yes. The agency told me that you'd like a demo of my skills. My clients usually let me feed the baby so that they can see how we bond." I look upstairs, searching for the trace of another soul. There seems to be no one in the house. "Will I be meeting the baby today?"

"No." Xavier takes a step closer to me, gazing down at my tits which are full to the point of bursting. "I want you to pump two bottles of milk for me to sample."

"I understand."

"Why don't you follow me to the nursing room?"

Yes, Daddy.

"Yes, sir."

I wonder when the kid is going to get here. The sky outside the window is dark, and I'm pretty sure it's going to rain soon. As I check out Xavier's sexy, toned butt that makes my mouth water with every step, I wonder if he is personally going to check the quality of my milk. Hot, rich men like him are so rare that I can't help but be drawn in by his dependable presence. My mind immediately conjures up an image of this sexy man pushing down my bra putting his hard mouth to my nipple and suckling my cream. God knows it's what I need, but not what I'm going to get.

Xavier walks ahead, and I notice the tail of his coat trailing behind him. With his long legs and black shirt, he looks good enough to eat. But he's so out of my league. He's like a Greek God carved from marble.

"Do you have a pump?" His voice is so silky and seductive. I want to drown in the fantasy of being taken naked by this man.

"Yes, sir." I shake my bag nervously. "I'm carrying one with me."

"Great." I follow him, awe-struck by every antique and painting that I cross. It must take a fortune to maintain this place.

"So, Anya, why did you decide to be a wet nurse?"

"I love nourishing people. It fills me with joy to know I can help someone by being my natural, feminine self. When I see babies get healthier and happier after drinking my breast milk, I feel so satisfied."

"That's..." He turns to me, his green eyes penetrating my soul. Why is his gaze so potent? It's like he sees right through me. His lips part, making me itch to kiss them. "That's admirable. Not many women would consent to feed kids other than their own."

"I like what I do. I enjoy my job." I try to keep the attraction from showing, digging my fingers into the straps of my bag to keep my wits.

"Do you have any kids of your own?"

"Not yet, but someday, I'd like to have lots of kids. I've always wanted a big family."

Xavier pauses, his hand resting on the wall for support. The way he watches me makes me feel like I've said something wrong. His eyes trail down my face to my lips, to my aching boobs before I notice that something is wrong. His breathing grows ragged like he's struggling to live.

"Are you all right?" I step forward, realizing that he's having an episode of something. His long legs bend, his face looking paler than usual. Cold sweat lines his features, his eyes glowing for a second. It's so otherworldly that I'm sure I imagined it.

"It's nothing." Xavier grabs his chest, massaging it. "I...I have a heart condition."

Immediately, I feel sympathetic. Is this the reason he retired to the country? His fingers struggle to grasp his shirt, his eyes shutting forcefully.

I place my fingers over him, noticing that they're cold. I can tell he's in pain and the woman in me wants to soothe him like a hungry baby.

"I'll do it." I lean in until the tips of my full tits are touching his chest. I place my hands on his chest, rubbing where his heart is. I mimic his movements, hoping he feels better. As I continue rubbing, I notice that the muscle contractions get more even. Xavier begins to breathe normally,.His fingers uncurl, grabbing onto me for support. My body reacts when his fingers dig into my fleshy arms, his face so close to my chest. I want to cradle him, beg him to put his mouth to my aching teats, and suckle my milk.

God, he makes my pussy so wet. I rub my legs together, just the simple act of touching my employer's chest and turning me on.

Xavier lays his hand over mine, his nose brushing my aching tits, "I can take it from here. Thank you." He curves his cool fingers over my hands and pulls them down, but he doesn't let go. We stare into each other's eyes, electricity sparking between us. I close my eyes, wanting him to kiss me, to grab my hips and have his way with my aching body, but my thoughts are cut short by a clap of thunder. Xavier lets go of my hand, gazing out of the nearest window.

Another clap of thunder resounds, and then, rain begins to pour. The pitter-patter of raindrops covers the roof, making the scene between us feel intimate. I shiver, watching the dark clouds stretch all around the house. It's like a horror movie, but I fight the chill claiming me. There's nothing to be afraid of. It's just Xavier and me here.

My billionaire employer drops my hand, clearing his throat. Without a word, he begins walking to the nursing room.

He leads me to a room at the end of the hallway and opens the door. It contains a double bed, a neat wardrobe, and a desk. The curtains are drawn over, providing privacy. The room looks like a historical servants' quarter. The stone walls and the echoes make it eerie. There's a smaller chandelier on the ceiling, but other than that, it looks pretty neat. Maybe Xavier has a maid come in every week to clean the place.

Leading me into the room, he says, "Please feel free to pump here. I'll be in my study when you're done."

I sit down on the bed, but when I turn, Xavier is still there. "Do you need anything else?"

"It's storming outside. I don't think the weather's going

to improve anytime soon. After you're done pumping, please stay the night." His voice makes goosebumps spark on my skin. Somehow, that practical decision sounds like an invitation to something forbidden.

"Sir?" I inhale, my pussy tingling at the thought of spending the night in close proximity to this sexy, older billionaire. My body is already heating, my bra pads wet thanks to all the milk my breasts have been releasing due to my aroused state.

"It's impossible to travel in weather like this. You can take the nursing room. The kitchen is stocked. Eat whatever you want. My staff are all off today, and I'm afraid I'm no good as a cook."

"I…thank you for your generosity. I'm sure I'll find something."

"Well, then, take your time." Xavier nods, stepping out of the room, but before he closes the door, he turns back, looking me directly in the eye when he says, "And Anya, call me Xavier."

With that, he closes the door and leaves me alone in the room, my heart in the throat and my body way too aroused.

CHAPTER 2
XAVIER

I want her.

Watching the flames burn in the fireplace of my study, my mind lingers on Anya. It's midnight, but I can't get the image of her curvy body, blue eyes, soft lips, and beautiful face out of my mind.

I shake a half-empty bottle of milk, watching the fire burning in the fireplace. Floor-to-ceiling bookshelves fill two walls of my study, adding charm to the Tallon manor. It's my favorite place in the world, and I've been recuperating here more often thanks to my health problem.

I gaze at the half-finished bottle of milk, and my mind suddenly goes back to the sight of Anya pumping milk in the afternoon. After she delivered two bottles of sweet cream to me, I immediately gulped one down, marveling at how fast it alleviated my weakness. Gone are the headaches and chest pains, and in its place is a newfound sense of vitality. I lick my lips, recalling the picture of my new, curvy milkmaid.

I feel a forbidden thrill pass through my body as I recall watching Anya take off her top this afternoon, revealing two gorgeous, milky melons clad in a nursing bra. Her curvy body made the heat in my groin flicker to life. When she took off her bra and released her massive udders, I forgot to breathe. My fangs grew out and I was dying to sink them in those fat, pink teats that were dotted with delicious cream.

I've always had a thing for women who want to be mothers. As the oldest vampire in a family of wealthy purebreds, it's my duty to continue the line. If it weren't for my illness, I'd have found a woman already, but none of the vampire women do it for me. No, I want a woman like Anya who is gentle and nurturing, her milkers filled with cream for her man. How she's managed to remain unattached for so long is a mystery. With her blonde hair, large blue eyes, and curves for days, she's exactly the kind of woman men thirst for. How does a man look at a woman like that and not dream of breeding her?

When she said she wanted kids, I was sold. She'd be the perfect mother, and with each passing moment, I want to wife her up more and more. It might be too early to fall for my wet nurse, but my vampire instincts tell me she's right for me.

I bring the bottle to my mouth, taking a sip of Anya's thick, creamy breastmilk. The moment the sweet liquid hits my tongue, I feel revived. The weakness in my heart dissipates, and my veins fill with power.

I've been like this since three years ago, ever since a mysterious illness claimed me.

You see, I have a problem.

Unlike other vampires who need blood to live, I need human milk.

Thanks to a genetic aberration that became apparent three years ago, my body needs breast milk to survive. I was born normal, able to hunt and drink blood, but three years ago, everything changed. My body began to reject blood, craving something else. I became weaker and weaker, and my parents thought I wouldn't live anymore. After a hundred years, my life seemed to be coming to an end.

I went to many doctors, but none of them could decode my vampire physiology. Coming from a family of pure-blood, wealthy vampires, it is my duty to continue the line and keep our lineage a secret. However, with my health problems growing and the media speculation surrounding my periodic disappearances, I thought I had no choice.

Until I sniffed breast milk one night.

I was stuck in a hospital, and I couldn't stop myself from turning. My entire body hurt, not having the energy to transform, and my heart ached. My chest pains are a consequence of my milk deprivation. Back then, I didn't know that human milk could cure me, but I scented it in the hospital. Nothing could stop me from tearing through the place, trying to locate the thing that called out to my senses like a siren's song. When I found it at the nursery in the form of a bottle of milk, I couldn't stop myself from drinking it all down. Two bottles later, my chest pains were gone. My sunken eyes had been revived, and my heart was beating again.

I couldn't believe it. For weeks, I'd been trying to find a cure, and it'd come in the form of breast milk. So, I began drinking breast milk every night, using my vampire doctor connections to secure some bottles. But soon, they ran out, and I realized that I couldn't keep sneaking in milk that belonged to the newborn kids. I had to find a regular source.

I tried everything— baby formulas, buying milk from nursing women, and even getting one of my vampire friends to produce milk—but nothing worked. I even tried hiring lactating women, but they were scared of me. The moment my fangs grew out, they ran away. If it wasn't for the NDA and the millions of dollars I paid to hush them up, I'd be the national laughingstock.

After my health took another downturn thanks to the erratic supply, I retreated to Tallon Manor. That's when I found out about Hercules Agency. I don't have high hopes, but I need this to work out if my health is to improve. And so, I contacted them.

That is how I came across Anya.

She's the first one I've had from Hercules, and so far, I love her milk. It's richer than anything I've tasted before and just one swig of it is so reviving.

Rain batters the glass window, the violent wind making the iron hinges creak. A rainstorm has broken out outside the window, but I can still hear the bats in the distance. My inner nature responds to the night's call, my nails growing out. I take another sip of milk, fueling my transformation. My eyes glow red, the hunter in me rising up in the dead of the night. I watch my fangs elongate in the antique mirror, a noisy grandfather clock pounding away next to it.

The Tallon manor is filled with secrets, with generations of forbidden liaisons, but I'm its best-kept secret—A vampire who awakens at midnight. Thunder crashes, drowning out every other sound. Lights flicker outside my study door, the narrow opening revealing everything. My muscles grow stronger with every swig of Anya's precious cream, completing my transformation. Lust surges through my veins, the hunter in me seeking out his milky prey.

I groan, craving the sensation of burying my fangs into Anya's heavy, milky melons and suckling her sweet cream straight from the source. I want to take care of her curvy body, fill that sweet pussy with my cock and drink her nourishing cream. She's so young, so giving, so innocent, that it makes me want to spoil her rotten. I've never met a woman who was a giver, but Anya is a giver. I know it just by looking at her. Breeding her ripe, lush body would be a dream.

As I drain the last drop of Anya's milk, I hear a loud crash outside. Instantly, I fly into action, dashing through the room with my superhuman vampire speed. My body passes through space like a bullet, shooting out into the hallway that overlooks the kitchen.

There, I find my prey.

My curvy wet nurse stands before me, her eyes wide with shock. Her hair is open, falling over her shoulders in an inviting gesture. But my eyes go straight to her nightgown that's parted in the middle, revealing her deep cleavage and outlining her delectable tits. The lust in my blood spikes at the sight of her wet teats staining the satin, her arousal molding against the fabric. The scent of sweet, nutty cream drives me insane, beckoning me like a black widow.

I can't stop my body from moving, from dashing at her and pinning her against the wall. Anya gasps, her heavy, firm tits leaking more milk as her mouth goes slack.

"What are you doing here?" My voice is gritty, My claws caging her.

"I...I...." Her eyes are large as saucers, her jaw quivering. I want to kiss that lush mouth. "What are you?"

"Anya..." I try to relax my hold, but my blood is hammering against my veins, desperate for her nourishing cream. "I need your milk." I gaze up at her, my face a little pale. "I'll tell you everything, but I need your milk to live."

"What?" She looks at me, her warm hands moving over my cold ones.

"I'm a vampire." I grab the wall, my voice strained. "I need milk instead of blood to live...It's because of a health problem I have." I want to get the words out fast because it's getting harder to stand here, surrounded by her warm body and the intoxicating scent of her titty cream. My head feels dizzy, my cock hard and throbbing for a taste of my milkmaid's sweet cream, straight from the source. "That's why I needed a wet nurse. It's the reason I'm staying at Tallon Manor. What happened earlier...that was because I'd been deprived of human milk for too long."

"So...you..." She gazes down, noticing the wet patches on the front of her gown. "The milk was for you."

I nod. "Does that make you uncomfortable? I know you usually feed infants." I try to pull away from her, but she grabs my hand. "If you want me to stop—"

"No." Her delicate fingers thread in my claws, and I lose myself in her large blue eyes. "I'm happy to feed anyone who needs my milk."

Damn, her giving nature undoes me. There's no explaining the irrational craving I feel for this sweet, beautiful, milky human. I can't explain my body's uncontrollable reaction to her like she's a match and I'm a powder keg.

With a grunt, I tear her nightgown open, the sound of my claws ripping fabric filling the night air. Thunder crashes outside the window, the sound of rain and tearing fabric filling the carpeted hallway. The lamplights flicker in the mansion, drawing attention to Anya's lush form. I want to take her to my study and slowly peel her clothing but the burning need inside me won't let me move. Her milky jugs bounce free, her teats swollen and wet with leaking cream.

"So beautiful," I palm her massive titties, making her moan. "I've never seen a woman as ravishing as you, Anya."

My tongue emerges from between my fangs, long and wet. The moment my tongue makes contact with her swollen, sensitive teat that's wet with cream, she gasps in pleasure. Anya arches her back, thrusting her nipple into my mouth. I close my lips around her peak and suck.

The first taste of cream straight from her udders is pure delight. I can feel my entire body responding to her, my hands holding her curvy form close. I fill my hands with her big hips and cup and squeeze her ass. "Yes..." she moans. "It's been so long since I've been touched by a man. Please, don't stop."

I sink my fangs into her sensitive nipples and she cries out loud as I suck milk like a straw through my vampire teeth. My mouth and teeth suction her achy titties as I palm her mounds soothingly. She shakes in my arms, my teeth pushing her toward an orgasm. Whenever a vampire sinks their teeth into a human's flesh, it arouses them.

"Good girl. You're doing so well, baby." I lick her hard peak, teasing her puffy areola before proceeding to suck mouthfuls of cream. It's like a dream, my curvy milkmaid and me enjoying this forbidden feeding in the hallway of Tallon manor, portraits and antiques overlooking us. I fist her skirt in my claws, pushing my hand under her skirt to touch her soft, thick thighs. I grind my erection into her covered pussy, needing the friction so bad.

"More..." Anya sinks her fingers into my hair, holding me close as I drain her titties. Every mouthful of sweet cream takes me to paradise. I want this woman so bad, it makes my body ache.

One hand slips behind her, cupping her sexy ass and kneading it as I press my groin to her stomach, letting her feel how hard I am. As my fingers reach between her legs, I feel her shaking against me. My fangs are stimulating an orgasm in my curvy milkmaid. Retracting my claws, I run a thick digit over her dripping folds.

"Fuck, you're so wet." I groan into her tits, intoxicated by the taste of her sweet cream and a touch of that wet pussy. My finger finds her little clit and rubs it.

Anya cries out, clinging to me harder. I pinch her clit between my fingers and she screams just as I retract my fangs from her drained tit. I lick her used nipple, pressing kisses onto her wet teat. "Shhhh, baby. I'm going to make you come before this night is over." She enjoys my tongue on her soft, sensitive flesh, making her feel desired.

"Xavier..." I kiss her milky mounds, finding her full breast and licking her leaking tip. "That feels so good." My fingers roll around her clit, making her lose control. I can feel how her tender flesh quivers. I put my mouth to her full teat and suckle a mouthful of milk. She arches her back in ecstasy, feeding me her nipple willingly. Her fingers thread in my hair, caressing them as she whispers, "Drink from me, Vampire lord. I hope my nourishing cream makes you feel better."

"Mmmm...It feels like heaven." I whisper against her milky nipple, sinking my fangs in hungrily. My fingers strum her clit until I know she's close to coming. Then, I slide up her slit and find that dripping cunt clenching for my fingers. "But it'd taste even better if you came for me." The moment I thrust one thick finger in, she shatters.

Anya's screams fill the hallway of the dark manor, drowning out the thunder. A wildfire of pleasure sweeps through her body, obliterating her sense of control. I can feel her tight little pussy clenching around my fingers, vacuuming them in. I thrust another finger in as I drain her other breast, filling my belly with veins with her titty cream that tastes so much sweeter because she's orgasming.

Anya's feet buckle, but I hold her up between my hard body and the wall. My fingers squelch in and out of her pussy as my tongue and fangs empty her tits, prolonging her orgasm. I'm so fucking hard, that I don't know how long I can keep doing this without coming. The desire for her is spreading through my body like a virus. I want to put my cock where my fingers are.

I lap up her milk like a starved man, loving how her soft, naked body presses against mine, and how her pussy drenches my fingers with her juices. I'm going to lick them clean and never forget the taste of my sweet milkmaid. I suck and suck until there's no more cream left in her fat, jiggly titties. My fingers are still inside her pussy when she stops coming.

Anya opens her eyes as I pull my mouth away from her breast. Her entire body is buzzing with an orgasm. "That was…I haven't come so hard in a long time." Her chest rises and falls with her breaths. There's a flicker of emotion in her eyes, something I can feel but can't quite name.

"You're gorgeous, Anya." I bring my cum-coated fingers to her swollen teat and gently massage her honey onto her tip. She moans when my tongue attacks her areolae, licking her honey and cream from it in slow, torturous circles. "Mmmm…I've never tasted cream as sweet as yours."

She holds me close to her breasts as I give her a little dirty TLC, soothing her teats. When I'm done, I look up into her eyes, knowing it's time to explain everything.

"So," she says, realizing it's time to define our relationship. "Do you want to tell me more about yourself?"

If only I could explain to myself what just happened. I've never done anything like this before, never felt a craving so bone-deep for a human. Yes, her milk attracted me, but I didn't make her orgasm for her milk. No, I want this woman, and I need to find out why. The need to take care of her, to make her happy is imprinted in my DNA.

I reach down and pick her up, carrying her to my study half-naked. "Mr. Tallon." She blushes, insisting I put her down. I love how solid her curvy body feels in my arms.

"Let me take care of you, Anya," I whisper, my lips brushing her cheek. "And then, I'll tell you everything."

CHAPTER 3
ANYA

There are few things that are as pleasurable as lying on a vampire's lap half-naked, his fingers rubbing salve on my sore nipples after a hot milking session. Fire blazes in the hearth of Xavier's study that looks like it's been plucked right out of a Victorian novel. With floor-to-ceiling bookshelves, a liberal use of wood, and a cozy, atmospheric vibe, it makes me feel like the heroine of a gothic novel. The milk has dried on my skin, leaving my nightgown a little wet, but I don't mind. But my mind is filled with everything Xavier just told me. He told me everything about his illness—how it began, how he's been struggling to secure a reliable supply of milk, and the frequent leaves of absence he's had to take from his job.

"I'm sorry about what happened earlier. Though I loved every moment of it, I shouldn't have attacked you like that. I hope you understand why I did that."

I nod, my heart sinking a little on realizing what we shared earlier was him reacting to a low supply of milk. After Xavier brought me in, he calmed down and apologized for his actions. The red blaze in his eyes is gone, yet, as he touches my breasts, all I can think of is him and the orgasm he gave me a few moments ago. "I now understand why you need a wet nurse." I swallow, trying to stop my pussy from dripping at his touch. "I promise, I won't tell anyone."

"Thank you."

Orange flames paint the whole room in a cozy, ethereal glow that makes me shiver, especially when I realize that it's raining outside. Inside here, it's hot, mostly because my hot, billionaire vampire employer has his rough, thick fingers circling my areolae, gently rubbing my nipples after a milking session. In all my years of being a wet nurse, I've never been taken care of so thoroughly. It feels so good to rest against Xavier's hard body, his long, hard legs caging my hips, his hard rod pressing onto my back as he kisses my hair.

Trying to fight the inappropriate attraction I feel for my employer, I ask, "Are there any other vampires like you?"

"None that I know of. I know all this sounds ridiculous. Until a few minutes ago, you didn't even believe in vampires."

"I do now."

When his body moved like a flash of light from his room and trapped me in the hallway, I felt a longing I'd never felt before. My body burned up, craving his mouth on my tits. Though I've been attracted to him since the moment I first laid eyes on him, the intensity of the first milking is something I've never experienced before. Did I feel that way because he's a vampire? Could there be another explanation for my intense response to Xavier Tallon?

"I would be happy to help you. I make loads of milk and you need it. I don't see why we can't continue our professional relationship." Though my mind is filled with questions, I know it is the right thing to do. Vampire or not, Xavier is sick, and he needs my milk. My heart aches for him, feeling his pain, his suffering like it were my own.

"You mean that?" His eyebrow quirks up, drawing attention to those sexy, full lips that were on my teats a few moments ago. My pussy clenches at the thought of him putting them on me again. This sexy billionaire vampire wants me, needs me, and I'd be crazy to say no. God knows I'm already halfway in love with him. His stable, reliable presence makes me long for more. However, the nurturer in me wants to help him. After he drank my milk, the color returned to his face. He looks gorgeous, with those bright green eyes and full lips, and part of me wants him to be healthy and safe, especially if I can help it.

"I do. I'd be happy to help, Mr. Tallon."

"Xavier," he corrects. "I know this is a lot to take in." Xavier gently palms my breasts, and I have a feeling he loves touching me. I love it when he touches me too, especially my milky mounds. When he sank his fangs into me earlier, I thought I'd come right on the spot. Before tonight, I never knew it would be so hot to be drained by a vampire, but it might be my new kink now. "I would understand if you wanted to leave. It can be a little overwhelming feeding an adult vampire. I need to milk you at least twice a day, and of course, I'd drink straight from the source." My belly flutters at the thought of Xavier's fangs suckling my milk. My nipples tighten under Xavier's touch. Having this sexy man drink from me twice a day sounds more like a sexual fantasy than a job. "I'll pay you whatever you ask for. Double, triple, quadruple..whatever it takes to make you stay. You will live in Tallon manor and your meals will be included."

"I don't need extra pay. I'm happy to help in any way I

can. You being a vampire or a fully-grown man doesn't change anything." I pause for a moment as our gazes lock. "I know you need my milk. I'd never deprive you of something you needed to live."

He inhales sharply, the corner of his mouth quirking up. "God, do you even know how rare you are? How is any man in his right mind supposed to resist a woman like you?"

"Mr. Tallon..." I blush. Hearing him say those words means so much to me. Though I know I'm only his milkmaid, fantasizing about being his woman is so tempting. "I'm not that much of a paragon. Besides, you're paying me to help you. It's just my job."

It sounds so wrong to say that. Xavier isn't my job. Not when I'm already catching feelings for him. Yet, I know that's all we can be. He might be attracted to me but he's a billionaire and I'm just a poor maid.

"That didn't stop my previous two maids from quitting. The media is going crazy, thinking I have a secret mistress and love child when I'm just sick. If I don't find a reliable supply of milk soon, I'll have to retire and that's not an option as a pureblood vampire." He inhales. So, Xavier is a pureblood vampire. I don't know what that means, but I sense that this is important to him. "Thank you for saving me. We'll draw up a new contract tomorrow morning."

"That...sounds good."

Lost in our conversation, I almost forget that I'm half naked, my tits out and Xavier's hand smoothing salve on them. "How does the salve feel?"

"It's soothing," I admit, not wanting to get out of his lap. I'm worried about his erection. If I turn around and unzip his pants, I can swallow his dick right now, but I don't know if that's appropriate. "But really, you don't have to go that far. I'll be fine by tomorrow morning."

I know we're only employer and employee, but there's something so gentle and loving about his manner that makes my heart melt. Without warning, a visual of me lying on this sofa, Xavier's hands around my pregnant belly, flashes into my mind. I shake my head, trying to dispel the thought, but every stroke of his sturdy fingers on my tits makes me long to take care of him and stay by his side.

"Please, let me take care of you," he says, moving to massage the cooling balm on my other tip. They tingle when he puts his fingers on them. "It's the least I can do after almost attacking you in the hallway and forcing you to feed me."

"You didn't force me," I say, feeling a shiver of arousal when his lips casually brush my head as he leans over. "I...wanted to be milked by you. I've...it's been a while since I slept with a man." I blush, regretting admitting my secret. "They're usually disgusted by a lactating female." He doesn't miss the pang of sadness in my voice as I deliver those words.

"They're all fools. I don't know how anyone would be able to resist your curvy body." He cups my breast and gently massages it. "This milk that you produce..." His hands slide down to my belly, caressing my bare skin, making my pussy flutter. "The ability to nurture life inside your body...You're a miracle, Anya. Men should worship at your feet because that's how mesmerizing you are in your fertile, feminine form. I, for one, have never met anyone as captivating as you."

I know he's just being nice, but his words unravel a frisson of need deep in my heart. For so long, I've wanted to be desired for being myself, for being a nurturer and a curvy woman, and this vampire right here is the first man who's given it to me. "And what about vampires?" I ask, my tone a little too teasing and inappropriate. "Do you think vampires might be interested in me? Maybe I just wasn't looking in the right place."

It's supposed to be a joke, but Xavier tenses up. His fingers pause their ministrations, and he pulls away, making my heart sink. His green eyes blaze red as he watches me. "Yes, I think vampires would be very interested in you."

His terse words make the blood pump to my core.

"And you?" I know it's wrong to ask. We just agreed to be employer and employee, yet against the rainstorm and the late-night fire, we're just a man and a woman. A very naked woman and a vampire man.

Without warning, Xavier pulls his hand back and gets up, leaving me on the couch. He walks away from me, shutting the salve bottle and placing it on his desk that's lined with papers. The scent of old pages fills the air as he turns his back to me. My heart sinks, knowing I crossed a line. I stand up too, pulling the flaps of my gown over my tits.

Just as I'm about to leave, I hear Xavier's low voice,

"This vampire is using every shred of self-control he has to stop himself from pushing you onto that couch and fucking you raw." He turns, his green eyes iridescent. My heart skips a beat, unable to take my eyes off my tall, sexy employer. A shiver travels through my spine. In a hoarse voice, he goes on, "I want to breed you do bad, Anya. I want to fuck that tight little pussy and feel it clenching around my cock when I fill you with my seed." A strangled cry escapes my mouth, but there's no stopping the intensity of Xavier's words. My pussy leaks, needing everything he said to be true. "Since the moment you walked into this house, I've been hard as a rock. So, don't tell me that your curvy mommy body isn't perfect, because I've never met someone who makes me crave so much by just existing."

The butterflies in my heart go all out. God, the way he looks at me like he wants to fuck me bare on this very couch and make me his, is more than I ever hoped for. Xavier is fighting his animal instincts, trying to make me feel safe.

"Mr. Tallon..." My eyes widen as he walks away, adjusting his black shirt.

He turns, offering only his broad, chiseled back to me which looks so sexy. With those long legs encased in black that that magnetic pull, his beauty is truly otherworldly. "Go to sleep, Anya. You have to wake up early tomorrow to feed me."

I obey, gathering the folds of my nightgown over my breasts and leaving the warm study. My feet feel unsteady as they walk to my room, his words echoing inside me. The dark, high-ceilinged hallways of Tallon Manor haunt me, making me aware of all the secrets this place hides.

Vampires. Who would've thought?

I touch my thudding chest, aching to feel where Xavier's hand has been.

It truly has been an extraordinary day.

I open the door to my room and sit in the darkness for several moments, trying to process everything that I just experienced. The awareness of Xavier sleeping a few doors down makes my body break out in gooseflesh. I can feel him viscerally like we're connected.

Even when I lie down on the bed, I can't sleep. His touch, his taste, and those words are fresh in my mind.

God, how am I going to last in this place for the next few months?

CHAPTER 4
XAVIER
ONE WEEK LATER—

"I don't want to marry Francesca," I tell my parents who are on a video call with me, pestering me about marriage again. "I know it's my duty as a purebred to produce heirs, but...not with Francesca."

Not when the woman I want is outside my door, humming as she cooks in the kitchen.

"Why not? She's the perfect girl for you."

Holding the phone in my hands, I put on earphones, covertly watching my new milkmaid cook herself dinner as my parents drone on. I'm too old to listen to them, anyway. Anya hums as she moves around, stirring pots in the kitchen. A warm, yellow light flashes overhead, enveloping us in a sense of domesticity as the sun sets outside the window. Anya's massive milkers are almost full, jiggling as she struts her curvy ass to and from the sink. It feels so forbidden, watching my maid like this, craving her as she goes about the most mundane of tasks.

It's been a week since we inked the contract, and she's been living with me ever since. I notice the little touches she's added to the manor, brightening up its dreariness with some flowers and fall colors. Most of all, she has brightened this place with her presence.

We've fallen into a routine. Every morning, I find Anya in the kitchen. She sits on the table and lifts her top, letting me drain her breasts. We do the same every evening after she eats her dinner, and every time I suckle her fat, milky titties, the need to breed her grows stronger. Every day, I have to dig deeper and try harder to control my natural instinct to claim my curvy milkmaid. It's no mystery that I'm falling for her. Her naturally caring nature appeals to me, and I love resting my face against her soft, milky mounds while she caresses my hair as I drink her nourishing liquid. The best part is that she's started to produce more, keeping those juicy milk jugs full all the time. A week of feasting on her milk day and night, and I'm brimming with health. Yet, no explanation seems forthcoming for my blazing attraction to her. All I know is if I don't act on it soon, I'll go crazy.

"You look healthy," my mother exclaims even as my father disapproves of me not producing a pureblood heir with Francesca. He left the business years ago, and I've been taking care of it ever since. My parents are purebloods too and they want me to continue the family line by producing heirs. "The new milkmaid is doing wonders for your health. I'd glad you found a reliable supply of milk."

"Hmmm." She's also working wonders for my libido, which I didn't really need help with. I've been taking too many cold showers, working out every opportunity I get to keep my thoughts off her, but nothing works. The moment my tongue touches her breasts, the can't stop needing to fuck her. Every time I milk her, I end up giving her an orgasm. Last night, I licked her pussy after milking her and made her come. I made an excuse that vampires get horny after milking, but I know my feelings for Anya are anything but professional. She's so responsive, and with each passing day, I'm falling deeper in love with her giving, nurturing personality. She takes care of chores around the house even though I hire a maid to do them. She also has been reading books about vampires in the library, trying to find out more about my race to help me better. Having her around the house makes me feel so much better. It's like things were always meant to be like this—me and her living together.

After telling her that I wanted to breed her a week ago, things have been rather quiet. A week with her and I'm brimming with health. However, I still haven't found the answer to my question. "Mom, I wanted to ask you something. What does it mean when you're intensely attracted to someone...kind of like a craving."

"You're in love, of course." She hums. "Are you talking about your fiancee?"

I roll my eyes. "She's not my fiancee." I notice Anya stiffen as she feels my eyes on her. When she turns around, she notices me watching her through the crack in my door. She inhales, her heavy breasts rising and falling. She's wearing a black tank top that hugs her massive milkers to perfection, revealing a delicious bit of cleavage that has me licking my lips. When she moves, I see her shorts that barely cover her sexy, thick legs, hugging her flared hips. It's a little tight between her legs, sinking into her pussy. I can smell how wet it is, and my strong instincts act up. That familiar thrumming in my blood is back again, my eyes flashing with hunger. Hurriedly, I turn back and close the door, fighting to suppress my urge. "I get hot flashes and my eyes turn red when I see her. I feel this deep need inside me...like my blood is on fire when she's near." The words spill from my mouth, as my parents notice my dilated pupils that are flashing.

"Xavier, are you okay?" My father steps in. "Who's that outside your door?"

"No one." I don't want them to know about Anya yet. Not until I figure out why her milk tastes so good. "I'm going to have to go now—"

"Wait," Mom interrupts, her eyebrows knit together in concern. "The symptoms you just described..." My parents are over two hundred but they look like thirty-year-olds thanks to their immortal nature. Their faces bear identical expressions as they turn to me. "It looks like you found your fated mate."

"What?" My heart stops for a moment. I know what fated mates are. Not all vampires have them, but some do. Hardly anybody in our social strata has a fated mate because marriages are arranged, but if mom is right... "Oh my god."

"Exactly my thoughts," dad says. "I...never realized you had a mate, but the things you described...that's what a vampire feels when they find their mate."

I drag a lungful of breath in. Everything suddenly makes sense. Anya is my mate. That's the reason I've been attracted to her since she arrived. That's also why her milk is so reviving.

"I have to go." I hang up on my parents, blood pumping through my body. I need her right now. I need her so bad. I'm tired of denying what's between us. Tonight, I'm going to mate my maid. I'm going to make her my partner.

Leaving the phone aside, I storm outside, the dark shadows of the manor following me like a dog. When I emerge in the kitchen, Anya turns around, startled by my footsteps. I stalk to her, my heart thudding violently as I gaze into the clear, blue eyes of my mate.

She's my fated mate.

Every instinct in my clamors to claim her.

"Xavier…" Her soft lips part and my gaze instantly trails to them. I want to kiss her so bad. "I didn't realize it was time for your feeding." Turning off the stove, she reaches for the hem of her tank, trying to pull it up, but before she can, I have her pressed against the counter, my hand around her waist.

"You have no idea how long I've waited for you." My intense gaze skewers her and I can feel her soft body surrender under mine. Her eyes close and her lips part, giving me the green signal to do what I've wanted for a week.

My lips meet hers and she moans, settling against my body. I pull her close, seating her covered pussy on my hardening bulge, and drinking in my mate's taste. Her lips taste so sweet, so pliant under mine. My mouth devours her, claiming her as mine. Her arms wind around my neck, her fat, soft tits pressing against the hard planes of my chest. We both know there's nothing professional about this kiss. I nibble on her soft lips, loving how she feels against me. The need to mate her and claim her buzzes through my body.

Heat sears through me as I thrust my tongue between those luscious lips. She tits her head, surrendering to the French kiss. I push one hand under her tank top, kneading her milky breast through her nursing bra. It's huge and engorged, making me want to tease her nipple. I unclasp the front flap, revealing her wet nipple to my fingers. The moment my padded thumb brushes over her areola, she moans into my mouth, our tongues making a sensual dance.

Ding dong.

The doorbell rings suddenly, interrupting our passionate kiss. My fingers are still on Anya's milky nipple, massaging the leaking milk into her sensitive tip. Her eyes go wide, inhaling sharply as I continue to kiss her. But the bell rings again, shattering our tender moment together.

I tear my mouth away from hers, reluctantly clasping her nursing bra and pulling my hand out of her tank top. I gaze down at her swollen lips and dilated pupils, wanting to claim her so badly. Pressing a kiss to her temple, I say, "I'll get the door." My fingers brush the exposed top of her arm, reassuring her that I'm going to continue what we started as soon as I've dealt with my unexpected visitor.

I reluctantly step away from Anya, marching to the front door with a frown. Anya follows me with soft footsteps. When I open the door, I see the most unexpected person standing on the other side.

With straight brown hair, a pair of silver eyes, high cheekbones, and a tall frame that looks like a supermodel, Francesca stands before me, removing her oversized sunglasses to take a look at me. I still tower a few inches over her, but in her heels and long legs, she's almost at par with me.

"I thought I'd pay my fiancé a visit." Her sultry voice echoes through the hallway, and I'm distinctly aware that Anya is standing behind me, her eyes wide as saucers. Francesca barges in, her eyes going straight for Anya.

Compared to her willowy, supermodel build, Anya is curvy and warm, her curves highlighted by her loungewear. "And who might this be?"

My self-proclaimed fiancee turns her intense gaze to me, quirking an eyebrow. Her eyes drift over Anya's impressive rack and she frowns. "You must be the new milkmaid. Your mom told me you'd found yourself a reliable supply of milk." Francesca sizes Anya up, gazing at her disdainfully. "I guess humans are good for something."

"Francesca, what are you doing here?" I move forward, standing between Anya and her. I know she makes Anya uncomfortable with her judging eyes and distaste for humans. Francesca is a pureblood too, which is why my parents want me to marry her.

"I wanted to confirm our engagement date." She casually gazes at Anya who is growing increasingly uncomfortable. Crap, she doesn't know I have a fiancee. "You see, I'm getting old and it's time we got married. My parents have been badgering me to set a date with you." Francesca's cool gaze travels over Anya. "I'd prefer to discuss our wedding arrangements without any servants around."

Her cruel words are too much. I turn to Anya and there's no missing the tears in her eyes. She turns her face away from me.

"Anya—" I reach for her hand but she moves back.

"I...I should get back to work." She hurries away before I can chase after her.

The moment I take my first step in her direction, Francesca says, "So, what's going on with that milkmaid of yours?"

Fury burns through my veins. I want to go to Anya and tell her that I'm not engaged to Francesca and never will be.

It's her that I want. However, before that, I need to get rid of Francesca.

I grab her wrist, dragging her forward. "Come with me."

～

"We're not getting engaged, Francesca. There was no need to announce yourself as my fiancee." I lean against my desk, watching my parents' favorite bridal option sipping blood for a wine glass. I keep some of it around in case of emergencies, though blood doesn't really do it for me.

"Why? Are you afraid your mousy little maid heard us?" She scoffs. "She has massive milkers, I'll give her that. I hope you're getting your money's worth. This one's already lasted longer than the others."

My fist balls up, tension traveling through my body. Anya is more than a wet nurse to me. Every time I drink from her, my feelings for her grow stronger. "Did you hear me? We're not engaged and we're never going to be."

"What's this about, Xavier?" She sighs like I'm a child throwing a tantrum. "Are you not ready to have kids yet? You're old enough. Our parents decided we'd get married long ago. There's no point in putting off the inevitable." She slithers across the room, her long legs on full display in her short skirt. Francesca is a supermodel by profession and she hasn't aged in several years. "You know as purebloods it's our duty to bear offspring with another pureblood. You and I have the best genes, I'm sure we'll have good-looking kids." Her cherry lips curve up in a serpentine smile that makes me squirm. I'm pretty sure she's here because she's insecure. Francesca has dated half the planet while I've been faux-engaged with her. We agreed to turn a blind eye to each other's actions until the wedding. However, meeting Anya has changed my perspective on marriage. I am no longer ready to have a marriage in name only. Having a cold, calculating woman like her next to me makes me crave Anya's warmth. With my curvy maid, I could have a real family: Real love, and real passion. Being born into an illustrious family with a strong lineage has made me realize the value of a nurturing, caring woman.

"I'm ready to have kids, Francesca, just not with you." My words are harsh, as I intend them to be. "Why did you come running to Tallon Manor? Was it because my parents told you I'd found my mate?"

The way she flinches tells me I'm right. "You can't do this to me, Xavier. I've waited for you all these years. You can't abandon me just because you're interested in some human."

"You haven't waited for me. You've been having fun with all those toys of yours. Both of us know this engagement is just our parents being stubborn."

Francesca's long, cherry nails curve around the wineglass, her eyes narrowing at me. She approaches me, and I stand tall. "So what? You want me to just let you go?"

"That's what normal people do," I tell her. "We don't love each other, and we never will." I know why I could never feel anything but a mild irritation for Francesca. It's because a loving, warm woman like Anya was always waiting for me. Looking at my fuming fiancee, I feel grateful to have escaped this horrible fate.

"We're too good for emotions. I mean, look at you. You're a hot vampire who has all the money and breeding in the world. Are you telling me you're giving this all up for some temporary flicker of emotion? I thought you were better than that."

It's just like her to twist everything to her benefit. I tolerated her for so many years, but I now know how wrong she is. With every insecure statement, she's laying all her faults bare. "Everyone wants love, Francesca. There's nothing great about living like a puppet. I'm old enough to know that and so are you. I won't follow through on my parents' plans for me. I will let them know that I plan to marry someone else. So if you're done berating me, I request you leave."

She places the finished wine glass on the table and takes a step away from me. She's smart enough to know I won't change my mind on this. We weren't officially engaged and now, we're never going to be.

"You're casting me aside because you found your fated mate," her words are low.

"We were never engaged. I'm not casting you aside. I'm just telling you how things are going to be from now on."

"Who is it?" she hisses, her smoky eyes narrow with hatred. No amount of makeup can conceal the ugliness of her heart. "Is it that stupid, fat maid of yours?"

I'm fine with her insulting me, but insulting my mate is unacceptable. I reach forward and grab her arm. "All right. You're done here." I drag her out of my room. "Anyone who insults my wife isn't welcome in my house."

"Wife?" She sputters. "Are you even sure she's going to accept a vampire like you? You're sick, Xavier. You need human milk to live. She'll never understand you. She'll never love an anomaly like you."

"Then, I'll just have to work harder to win her love." Her words don't make any difference to me. Even if I have to spend the rest of my life convincing Anya to be with me, I'd rather do that than settle for someone like Francesca.

I drag her to the door and let go of her arm. Opening the door wide, I show her the way out. "Goodbye."

Sputtering, she walks out. "You're going to get bored of that ugly cow and then, you'll come running back to me."

I watch her get into her car and drive away, and once she's gone, I walk to Anya's room. I've got to make sure she's all right.

CHAPTER 5
ANYA

I can't do this.

Tears streaming down my face, I stare at my reflection in the mirror. It's been twenty minutes since Xavier's hot, supermodel fiancee arrived, and I've been a mess ever since. My heart clenches at the memory of our kiss in the kitchen, at all the feedings we've had over the past week and the conclusion is clear—I'm in love with Xavier. Ever since the first time I laid eyes on him, I'm been falling deeper in love with him. Having him pressed against my chest, lovingly draining my mounds as I caress his hair is the best part of my day. I love nurturing him, love how he makes me feel good about myself, and appreciates my natural, feminine nature.

"You're so stupid," I tell myself, wiping the tears away. "He's out of your league."

While I was busy falling for Xavier and fantasizing about having his babies, I forgot that he's a billionaire and hot as sin. Of course, he'd never be interested in a woman like me. Francesca with her pureblood lineage, supermodel body, and wealth is a much better match for him. What could I even offer him except my love?

I hear footsteps outside the door and then, there's a knock. Before I can hide my crying face, the door opens with a thud, and Xavier stands on the other side. My heart aches at the sight of his tall, sexy form, hanging over the doorframe like a long shadow. How was I supposed to resist developing feelings for him? The nurturer in me just wants to heal this vampire and be by his side.

"Anya." His deep voice resonates in my bones. Xavier stalks in, shutting the door behind me. Instantly, his eyes are on my face and there's no hiding the fact that I've been crying. I hurriedly blot away the tears, trying to look normal, but it's no good. Xavier sinks onto the mattress next to me, brushing my tears with his thumb, making my pussy and heart flutter at the same time.

"I'm sorry, baby." His voice is pure seduction. He puts his mouth next to my ear, licking the shell as he dries my tears. My body is already reacting to his touch, my tips leaking milk and my entire body aching to fall into his embrace.

"Your fiancee—"

"She's gone now, and she won't be back." He kisses the shell of my ear, his fangs emerging to tickle my cartilage. It sends a shiver through my body, making me moan. "I'm sorry you had to put up with that."

His every kiss, every lick is making me forget who I am, but I know there can't be anything between us. Not when he's engaged to another woman.

"I can't do this," I tell him, backing away from his touch. Xavier's green eyes are dark with hunger as he gazes at my face. I wrap my hands around my body, and the tears begin to flow again. "I..know you need my milk but...I can't do this anymore. I'll find a way to pump milk and get it to you...I...I'm sorry."

I expect Xavier to be shocked, but instead, he puts his strong, big arms around me and envelops me in a warm hug. My body reacts on its own, slipping into his lap as he holds me close. My legs straddle him, my breasts pressing against his chest, feeling his erection under me. I need to cling to him so badly like he's the only one who can make me feel better. The need to be near him defies logic. "Shhh, baby, don't cry. Tell me what's wrong." He kisses my wet cheek, tasting my salty tears. I can't stop crying. It feels like my heart is breaking.

"I...I love you," I say between sobs. "I know I'm not good enough for you. You're engaged to a gorgeous woman and I'm sure I'm nothing more than a convenient supply of milk, but...I can't just be your milkmaid anymore. I tried but—"

Xavier's hand slips under my tank top, caressing the naked skin of my back as he lets me cry against his chest. His shirt is so soft, reminding me how luxurious it feels to touch him. "Anya, Francesca, and I are not engaged. I told her that after you left. Our parents have been wanting us to get married, but I assure you, I have no intention of following through." He presses a kiss atop my head. "Not when there's someone else I'm in love with."

"What?" Oh my god, is there another woman? Is he trying to let me down gently? I look up into his mossy gaze, magnetically drawn in by his seductive good looks. It's not just his face, but his aura, his energy, his very being that I feel connected to.

"I'm in love with you, babygirl." He kisses my temple.

"What?" My heart stops, unable to believe what I just

heard. Hearing him call me 'babygirl' makes my pussy drip. "You...you love me?"

"I told you I've been attracted to you ever since I saw you, but I couldn't understand this intense, inexplicable bond between us. I needed time to figure out what was going on." Xavier's fingers reach up, unclasping the back of my bra. I whimper when my achy, milky melons are set loose. Relief floods my chest, and the longing to have Xavier's mouth on my tingling teats increases. Xavier leans forward, pressing a quick kiss on my lips before he says, "You're my mate, Anya."

"Mate?" I blink, my tears pausing. I don't understand what he means.

Xavier slides his big hand under my bra, cupping and palming my udders lovingly. "Fated mates," he says. "You see, some vampires have fated mates, a person they're destined to be with. Those lucky enough to have mates are considered rare, and it seems that I'm one of the lucky ones."

When his thumb brushes my bare, swollen nipple, I close my eyes in ecstasy. "So, you mean...we...I...?"

"You're the one for me, baby. You complete me in ways no one else can. It's no wonder that your milk feels so sweet. I can always feel you, even when you're not next to me. There's never a moment when I don't long for you, that I don't crave your body. When we're together, I feel like we're connected by an invisible thread. Everything with you is so much more intense."

My jaw drops open. "That's exactly how I feel."

Xavier smiles. "That's because we're fated mates. You're the woman I was born to love, Anya. I wanted to be sure before I mated you, babygirl."

Milk leaks from my tips onto his fingers. My pussy

clenches for him, for my vampire mate. I know what he said is true. "We're perfect for each other. Our bodies are the perfect fit, and our souls were meant to find their way to each other."

I can feel his words deep inside me, filling my heart with a mix of joy and sentiment. Tears stream from my eyes, touched by what he told me. Xavier and I...we're meant to be. My coming here wasn't a coincidence. It was fate.

"Oh my god...I can't believe this." Through my tear-stained eyes, I see Xavier's blurry face. He's so beautiful, those chiseled features and hard jaw make my heart ache. "So, we're...You..."

"I love you, Anya." He rocks me against his erection, rubbing circles around my aching, milky tips with his thumbs. "I'm done fighting my feelings for you. I need you now, baby." I can feel the proof of his arousal, his hands touching the most intimate parts of me.

"Tell me you want this." His voice is a growl, his thick rod pressing against my fertile stomach. The scent of my nutty, sweet cream fills the air.

My plump lips part, saying the words I've wanted to say since I got here. "Fuck me, Daddy."

Xavier's hands stop playing with my tits and reach for the hem of my tank top, pulling it and my bra over my head. I raise my hands as my mate relieves me of my clothes. My fat, milky melons bounce free, the tips thick and elongated with beads of white milk clinging to the surface.

"Mmmm...these titties drive me mad." Xavier pushes me on the bed, climbing over me. His hands palm my overflowing breasts kneading them gently to begin the flow of milk. He touches the tip of his tongue to one aching teat and I moan loudly. It feels so good to have that wet, thick tongue rolling over my nipples, giving me the relief I so badly need. "You're engorged, babygirl. Do you need Daddy to drain those titties?"

"Yes, Daddy," I cry out.

"Mmmm...You love calling me Daddy, don't you?" He licks my nipple a little more before capturing it in his mouth. He licks it thoroughly, arousing and priming me before letting go. "You're so beautiful, Anya. I wanted to fuck you every time I drained these beautiful, milky mounds. I always knew you belonged to me."

I skewer my fingers in his hair as he lays his face on my breasts, palming and kneading my tits as his mouth licks my nipples in turns. He grazes his fangs against my areolae, preparing me for an intense milking as he runs his tongue all over my puffy, pink teats. "Oh my god...I love it when you milk me...it makes me feel like I belong to you. Everyday, I waited for our milking session, longing to nourish you with my cream and share this intimacy. I never wanted it to end. I'd make myself come after returning to my room, aroused from how your fangs felt on my breasts. When you touched my nipples and applied salve after the milking I..." I pause as his mouth covers my teat.

"What did you think, babygirl?" He asks, waiting for my answer.

"I imagined myself pregnant with your babies, you caressing my swollen stomach as you soothed my titties next to the fire. It was just a fantasy...but I longed for it to be true."

"God, baby, you're so perfect." Xavier kisses my tip before he swallows my thick nipple and sucks hard. Letdown hits, tearing a pleasured cry from my throat.

Xavier sinks his fangs into my swollen teats, drinking from my ducts like a straw. My sweet cream fills his mouth, running down his chiseled jaw.

"Daddy!" Ecstasy spirals through my body traveling down my belly to my hot core. Every time he sinks his fangs in me, I almost come.

I caress his face, sliding my hands down his neck to feel his skin. He's warm, his belly filling up with my milk and his countenance growing stronger. I love it when he lets me nurture him with my boobs. I silently lay on the bed, his body over me as he drains my breast ceaselessly. I've been engorged for so long that it feels wonderful to be milked. As the tension drains away from one tit, the pulsing in my pussy grows. I spread my legs, my panties drenched and forming a wet spot on my shorts. Xavier's thick bulge rests on my stomach, making me needy for more.

Xavier pulls his fangs from my breast, draining the last few drops of my liquid gold with his mouth. He kisses all over my breasts as his fingers reach lower and pull down the waistband of my shorts. He slips his fingers under my panties, sliding them over my pussy, and groans loudly against my boob. "Fuck, baby, you're so wet." He pulls away from my breast with one final lick. His fingers strum my clit, making my wet, aching bead all hard and needy. My pussy clenches around the air, and Xavier thrusts one finger into my core, testing it. He groans as I feel tension building in my core. "Baby, you're so wet, my finger slides right in. It looks like it's time to mate you."

Xavier pulls back, popping the buttons of his dark shirt and discarding it on the floor. He looks down at me, my naked breasts heaving up and down. I fumble with his belt, pulling it off to find the button of his trousers. He puts his big hand over mine and uses my fingers to pull his zipper down. Then, he pulls his pants off, leaving him only his boxer briefs. He gets off me, pulling them down and then, he's naked.

I gasp as his heavy cock bounces free. It's hard and leaking pre-cum from the tip. There's no missing how big it is and how hungry he is for me. Veins throb all over the surface of his shaft, and I ache to feel them inside me. He puts his hand around his cock and gently strokes it.

"Open your legs, Anya. Let Daddy see that pretty pink pussy dripping." I open my legs wider, my mouth watering at the sight of his massive cock in his hand. My pussy clenches at the thought of having that virile monster inside me, pumping me full of Xavier's cum. Xavier strokes himself until he's harder, before climbing back on top of me, watching my full breast leak in arousal. He lets go of his shaft, placing his meat on my thigh while he uses the hand that stroked his cock to touch my leaking nipple. "Your cream tastes so sweet when you're aroused, babygirl. I'm going to taste you when you come around my cock."

My entire body heats up in response to his dirty words. I spread my legs wider, feeling his thickness rubbing against my slick folds.

"Daddy, I need your cock," I whimper, grinding my wet pussy on his bare cock. "Please, put it inside me."

Xavier grabs his thick shaft and positions the mushroom head that's wet with pre-cum over my cunt. He drags it all over my folds, lubricating me with his pre-cum, and I love how every slide of his baby-making organ gets me hotter to take his seed. He rubs it over my clit, stimulating me. With every drag of his penis over my little bead, he's making sparks explode inside my belly.

"I'm going to fuck you bare and come inside you, Anya. I'm going to mate you and breed that curvy body. Daddy's gonna make you a milky mommy for real." He pushes the head of his cock over my hole and thrusts. I cry out loud as he fills me to the brim, stretching my walls. His loud grunt as my tight pussy grips him reverberates through the mansion. The darkness outside is contrasted with the heat spreading between us.

"Daddy!" I cry out as he leans over and puts his mouth to my full breast. He closes his lips around my teat and suckles a mouthful of milk. My pussy ripples around his cock, begging him to move.

"Fuck, babygirl you're so tight." He pulls out almost all the way and slams back in, making my titties jiggle and spray milk into his mouth. He suctions my breast greedily, licking and teasing my sensitive peak as he moves inside me. He grabs my hips and pistons into me, his thick cock stretching me and filling me up. It feels so good to be plugged up by his fat dick, mated to a vampire. His thrusts get harder and deeper, grinding against my G-spot before touching the opening of my womb, where I'll nourish his seed. "Mmmm..." He pulls his mouth from my breast, licking the overflowing cream. "You're perfect for me, baby. I'm going to pound that pussy raw and leave it all swollen. By the time Daddy's done with you, you won't be able to walk straight."

He drills my pussy with his cock, his balls slapping against my ass. He is as needy as I am, craving the mating we've been hurtling toward since our initial meeting. With every scrape of his cock inside my fleshy channel, he's driving me insane, pushing me closer to my climax. My whole body is on fire, my pussy burning for his seed. When

Xavier sinks his fangs into my milky ducts and sucks, I shatter with a scream.

"Daddy!" An orgasm sweeps over me, making my body explode. The intense climax forces me to surrender to a sensation I've never known before. His steel pole fucks me ruthlessly, disappearing in and out of my sex. My pussy spasms around his swollen cock, my womb aching for his hot seed. "Oh my god..." Our joining is so powerful, so intense that it takes my breath away. Xavier's mouth tugs and pulls on my nipple as he gorges on my fresh cream like a starved animal. The wet sound of his mouth sucking on my teats turns me on. His narrow hips rhythmically thrust into my sex, prolonging my orgasm. I run my hands all over his muscles back and chest, feeling every inch of hot skin. I need him so bad. He's the only one who can satisfy the craving in me.

"Baby, your pussy is choking Daddy's cock. You're gonna make me come," he grunts, fucking me harder as the final droplets of cream fill his mouth. I squirt pussy juices all over his pole, loving the way his fat balls filled with seed slap on my ass, promising to explode anytime. Every time he moves in and out of me, my brain short-circuits, seeing stars. I wrap my legs around him, sinking my heels into his ass to grab his cock tighter.

Xavier's body goes tense, his eyes lighting up and turning red as his orgasm takes over him. With one final thrust, he explodes inside me, painting my walls with hot, thick ropes of cum. His growl fills the air, our pleasured voices screaming and panting in the empty mansion.

"Anya....baby, you're mine." He licks my breasts, resting his head on the creamy pillows of fat, and murmuring into my skin. His girthy cock plugs me up, and it feels so good to be filled with his seed. My silky walls massage his shaft, feeling the veins throb as he empties his balls inside my womb. It's the ultimate mating. The perfect joining.

Another orgasm blazes through my core like wildfire, consuming everything. His touch is possessive as he sinks his fingers into my hips that'll soon be swollen with his baby. Boiling hot cum fills up my channel, his cock pulsing inside me as I shiver and moan with need. We're both coming together, mated, and joined in the most meaningful way. He's mine now, and I'm his. My body surrenders to its rightful owner, riding out the waves of bliss together.

After what seems like an eternity, we finally slow down. Xavier's panting, naked body moves over mine, his cock going soft inside my pussy that's filled with cum to the brim. His sweaty skin moves against mine, and I groan in pleasure.

"Babygirl, you were perfect. God, I've never come so hard before." He kisses my face, the tears long dry. With him inside me, my body feels all warm and fuzzy, like it's in its most natural state.

"Me too," I confess. "I'm so glad that…it was with you."

My mate looks down on me, his eyes filled with lust and tenderness. His lips dip down, touching mine, and blanketing me in a hot kiss. I surrender to my vampire Daddy's kiss, feeling him everywhere like he's part of my blood. The bond we share is so deep, so intimate, that I can't help but bow in humility to its power.

When he pulls away with a final wet kiss, I can barely breathe. Xavier pulls out of my pussy, kissing my temple. "I'm going to keep you next to me, Anya. Daddy's going to breed that pussy day and night until you're knocked up. I can't imagine being away from you ever again. Baby, this curvy, milky body belongs to Daddy now, and I'm going to take good care of it."

"Xavier..." I can't believe this is really happening. Just days ago, I was fantasizing about this man, and now, he wants me to be his. "I...There's nothing I want more than to be by your side, nurturing you and our babies. Bringing you pleasure makes me so happy."

He touches every inch of my body, his mouth kissing my shoulders, and his fangs grazing that sensitive spot between my shoulder and neck. My tits are tender, my tips glistening and swollen with his saliva. I can still feel him in my pussy.

"I'm so lucky to have found you, Anya." He kisses my shoulder. "A nurturing, loving woman like you is so rare in this world. When I think about not having you, my heart feels bleak. I'll provide for you and our children so that you can be your natural, feminine self, and just focus on nurturing your family, babygirl. Daddy will make you come every day, and keep those milky mounds drained and happy."

"Daddy..." My eyes fill up with tears again, and this time, Xavier kisses my eyelids. "I...you're everything I've ever wanted. Before I met you, I never thought anyone would love me for being my nourishing, motherly self, but you love me just as I am."

"Are you kidding me? I love your curvy body so much that I want to keep it curvy and swollen with babies all the time and keep those mounds filled with milk. You're going to have to produce a lot, baby, because you've got one hungry vampire and lots of babies to feed."

"I don't mind," I smile. "Taking care of you and our babies will make me so happy." I revel in his attention and love as he tenderly kisses me all over, his mouth moving over my belly. "I'm going to tell everyone tomorrow, and then, we'll have an official ceremony." He caresses my stomach with his big hands. "I hope you're all swollen with our baby by then."

My pussy contracts at his words, needing them to be true. I caress his hair as he rests on my belly which is filled with his seed. This feels so perfect.

We fall asleep like that next to each other, and I feel at home with my mate's head resting on my body.

CHAPTER 6
XAVIER

"Good morning, baby." I wake my mate up with a good morning kiss to her wet pussy. She moves in bed, her thick thighs bracketing my face. Anya's beautiful blue eyes open and she groggily looks down at me between her legs.

"Xavier?" Her eyes open wider as my warm breath ghosts her tender pussy. Last night, we made love twice, and by the time I was done, she was sore, her belly full of my cum. I slept with her warm, curly body wrapped in my arms, and I've never slept better. However, that also means I woke up this morning with a hard rod, and the insatiable need to please my mate. Anya's massive milkers are full again, rising and falling with each breath. She eyes me from over her fat mounds that I'm going to drain once I've made her come.

My hands sink into her curvy hips, intoxicated by the scent of her musky pussy. "Did you sleep well last night?" My tongue shoots out, licking her wet slit from clit to cunt. Anya's legs shake.

"Y-yes..." She clutches the bedsheets, her body

responding to my lick. I lick her swollen folds which are all tender and responsive to my tongue. Her pussy begins to leak at once, responding to my tongue. My fangs emerge, lightly teasing her most sensitive flesh. "Mmm..."

"I thought I'd check on your pussy today. How do you feel?" My tongue licks her sore spots, circling her wet cunt.

"Sore," she admits. "But your tongue feels so good, Daddy."

"I'm going to make you feel even better, babygirl." I flick her hard clit with my tongue, burying my nose in her pussy and smelling her sweet, aroused scent. When my fangs lightly graze her bundle of nerves, her hips arch and I use my hands to hold them in place.

"Mmmm..." She moans, pushing her fingers into my hair and holding my head between her legs. I sink my fingers into her curvy, round butt, loving how all that fat feels, and pull her pussy close to my nose, continuing to torture her nub. "I love waking up to mornings like this."

I capture her little bud between my lips and suckle on it. My tongue and teeth play with her clit, pulling on her hot button until she's crying out for a good fucking. My tongue slides down her pussy, and without warning, I push into her quivering hole.

"Daddy!" Her cries fill the bedroom as I thrust my thick tongue in and out of her well-bred pussy, grinding against her G-spot. Wet sounds of me eating pussy fill the air, my fangs grinding against her soft folds and supple ass cheeks.

She orgasms instantly, coming with screams that fill up the quiet manor. This place never felt better than when Anya is here, filling up the mansion with her musical sex sounds. Her pussy spasms around my tongue, drenching me in her honey. I thrust in and out of her cunt, prolonging her orgasm and tasting her sweet release until she's wiped out.

Pulling my tongue out of her pussy, I climb on top of my mate's sweaty, curvy body, loving how her naked, engorged tits look in the first light of dawn. I press a dirty kiss on her soft mouth and immediately, her hands go around me, tasting her release on my lips. The kiss is hot and intense, and when Anya feels my cock pressing against her belly, she comes up for air. "That's quite a morning." Her fingers skim down my body, wrapping around my swelling cock. Gently, she strokes me and I offer her a tight groan. Her soft fingers feel heavenly on my bare shaft, tracing the veins on my velvety skin. She circles her thumb around my tip, rubbing the pre-cum all over.

"I've wanted to touch your big cock ever since I saw it last night." She begins to move her fingers up and down, her knuckles bumping against my tight balls that are aching to spill on her massive milkers. She grips me a little tighter, moving up and down in rhythm.

I palm her fat tits, looking forward to milking her. My mouth kisses one nipple and she jerks in response, grabbing my dick tighter and making sensation build in my belly. "Daddy wants to spill all over your milky tits, babygirl." I softly massage her breasts, leaning over to lick a drop of cream that emerges.

"Daddy..." She loves it when I let her nourish me and lavish attention on her overflowing udders. I put my mouth to one tit and suck hard. Sweet cream fills my mouth as my mate's hands continue pumping my cock. I can feel heat trickle all over me, the ball of tension at the base of my spine needing to explode. She pumps me hard and fast, as I empty her tits, taking one drag from one milky mound before alternating with the other. Her letdown makes her pussy buzz and when she grinds her bare pussy against my cock and massages my balls, I come.

Pulling away from her tits, I rain hot ropes of cum all over her breasts, showering her with my seed. The sensation of hot seed spilling over her tender boobs makes Anya hot and she continues to milk my dick, pumping hot cum all over her body. By the time I stop coming, my cum is all over her body, covering her pillowy tits, her belly, and her shapely hips.

"Mmmm...I love the sight of you covered in my cum." I rub it into her belly. "It lets everyone know you're mine, baby."

She loves being massaged with cum and smiles up at me. "I wish we could stay in bed forever. I love everything you do for me, Xavier. It's like my body was made to be used by you."

"It was, baby. This ripe womb is soon going to be carrying my babies." I rub my cream all over her soft midsection. "And these titties were created to feed my hunger." I cup her breasts and squeeze letting droplets of milk leak out. I press my finger over her squishy nipple, painting little circles on it. "You're mine, Anya. This sexy, curvy body belongs to me now and I'm going to take really good care of it." I press a kiss to her wet titties, letting her know how much I love them. "Now get out of bed, babygirl. It's time for my morning feeding."

∽

"Wow, this is amazing." Anya stares at the tableful of food I cooked up for her while she was resting. After I ate her pussy and milked her, we showered together, and I had the chance to rub soap all over her sexy body and care for my babygirl. Once she gets pregnant, I'm going to shower with her all the time.

After the shower, Anya fell asleep. She was tired after making love last night, and I wanted her to get some rest. It also gave me the time to get everything in order for my romantic proposal. I am sure Anya is the woman I want to marry, the one I need to have by my side. She is my mate, and I want to wife her up before anyone gets in the way.

"You...when did you get these flowers?" Anya stares at the display of red roses and white flowers that are arranged at the center of the long dining table. Chandeliers are lit overhead, the long windows of Tallon Manor making it look like we've gone back in time. The paintings and wood paneling add character to our romantic dinner. I wanted to make our proposal even more special, but the need to ask her to marry me as soon as possible left me with only this option. If it were up to me, I'd have asked her to be my wife while she was in bed, covered in my cum, but Anya deserves a special, romantic gesture.

"I ordered them and they arrived earlier. I wanted to surprise you."

Anya looks hot in a black dress that she got. The body con dress with thick straps hugs her full figure, making her look like a hot mommy. Any other woman would look plain in this dress, but Anya looks mesmerizing, her curves taking centerstage. Her cleavage is so lickable and once I'm done with this proposal, I'm carrying her to my bedroom and taking off that dress.

"You look ravishing." I press a kiss to her cheek, putting my hand on her back to guide her to her seat next to mine. The table has twenty-four chairs, but I'm going to keep her close to me.

I serve her the food I prepared, wanting to keep things

intimate without any house help. As Anya eats, I watch her, observing her breasts swelling up with milk. I keep my fingers threaded in hers, feeding her the steak when she protests she can't eat with one hand.

"All this is so romantic. I don't think I've ever been courted before."

"This is just the beginning," I tell her. She has no idea how much I plan to spoil her once we're married. I wipe her lips when she finishes eating, licking the remnants of her saliva and the steak from my fingers. "I love watching you eat." Good thing I'm going to get to watch it for the rest of my life.

"Really?" She leans back as I give her a piece of the chocolate cake I ordered. "And I love looking at my handsome vampire Daddy." Her fingers press against mine. "This is all like a dream."

Yeah, being with a woman like her, who is so giving and open, is a dream. Anya attacks the dessert, determined to enjoy every moment of our at-home date.

When she moans at the pleasure of tasting a delicious chocolate cake for dessert, I know it's time to pop the question. Sated and full, she leans back on the chair, smiling at me, rubbing her full stomach. "That was quite a feast. Thank you, everything was delicious. I don't think I've ever eaten such amazing food."

"Baby, you're a special woman and I wanted to make this moment special for you." I reach into my pocket and pull out a velvet box. It's the ancestral ring that has been handed down in my family for generations. I inherited this one from my grandmother, and it was always meant to belong to my wife. I open the box and a huge sapphire ring framed with diamonds stares back at us, taking my mate's breath away. "It's time to tear up our contract and make a new one. One that says you're my wife." Anya gasps, her blue eyes widening in surprise. I get off the chair and kneel on the floor, holding up the ring to my mate. "Will you marry me, Anya? Will you make me the happiest man on earth by being my wife?"

Instantly, tears fill her eyes. The scenery goes blurry before her eyes as she gazes up at me. "Xavier..."

'You're the one I want to spend my life with, babygirl. I want to make you happy, keep your belly filled with babies, and have more such romantic moments with you. When I wake up in the morning, I want you next to me, feeding me with your nourishing cream and reminding me how much I love your body." I'll never forget how beautiful her teary eyes look in this moment.

She drags in a breath, wiping the tears from her eyes. "Are you sure? I mean, it hasn't been that long since we met." She puts her hand to her heart. "Though I love you... You're a billionaire and all I can offer you is my love." There's a hesitation in her manner, a sense of doubt I want to wipe off her face.

I take her hand and kiss it. "Baby, do you have any idea how rare you are? Your love is the most valuable thing in the world. I can't believe I was lucky enough to find you in a world filled with cold and calculating women. Anya, your love is all I need. Please, babygirl, say yes. Say you'll be my wife."

Tears stream down Anya's face as she leans forward. "Yes," she says. "I can't believe I get to be your wife. From the moment I arrived in this manor, I've been fantasizing about being more than your milkmaid and...I can't believe this is really happening."

"You better believe it's real," I tell her. "Because there's no way I'm letting go of you now that I've found you." I pull out the ring and slide it onto her ring finger. It's a tight fit, but we'll get it altered later. For now, I want to ravish my future wife.

The ring in her finger, she stands up and I put my arms around her soft, fleshy body, holding her close to me. Our lips meet in a searing kiss that seals our promise. I taste my wife's sweet flavor, devouring her pretty mouth. She's mine now. Anya's hands curve around my waist as I press her closer to my body, consuming her like oxygen. My hands brush against her full udders, and Anya moans with pain. My milkmaid needs a good, filthy milking. Just when I'm about to tear my mouth away, I hear a loud gasp.

Instantly, Anya and I break away and turn to find two people standing at the helm of the dining room. I take in the sight of my parents. My mom, a willowy, raven-haired beauty with red lips, wears a powder blue skirt suit and pearls, her eyes firmly fixed on Anya who is pressed close to me. My father, a blonde-haired man in a black suit, raises his eyebrow at me.

"I thought we'd pay you a visit after your call yesterday." My mother's eyes turn to Anya. "Francesca told me you called off the engagement, and I was worried." There's no emotion in her gaze, and I realize this is a time as good as any other to announce our good news.

"Mom, Dad, this is Anya." I take her hand in mine, holding it up so that they can see the family ring on her fingers. "My future wife." Anya breathes nervously, turning to me. I take her hand to my mouth and kiss it in a show of intimacy. "I just asked her to be my wife, and she agreed."

"What?" My father leans forward. "But..."

"We're fated mates," I tell them. "You know what that means."

"When...did you meet her?" My mother takes in Anya's

curvy, lactating form and her eyebrows scrunch together. "Is she...your...wet nurse?"

"She was my wet nurse," I tell them. "Now, she's my fiancee." I gaze into Anya's beautiful eyes, sensing her nervousness. "Why don't we all go sit down somewhere. I'm sure you want to get to know Anya."

"That...that'd be great." Mom leads the way, and Anya and I follow, my hand always in hers for reassurance. This isn't how I wanted to introduce her to my family, but now that they're here, I can't wait for them to see what a gem Anya is.

We all sit down on the couch in the living room, my parents facing me.

"Is she the reason you broke off your engagement with Francesca?" Mom asks.

"We were never engaged," I tell her. "She only wanted to use me to bolster her image." I hate that they're still talking about Francesa, not Anya, so I divert the conversation. "Anya here has been helping me with my illness. I never thought I'd find someone as loving as her, but it looks like fate had different plans."

Anya offers me a watery smile.

"Yes, the milkmaid." My father sits back. "She's a human, isn't she?"

My fist tightens. I don't like that they're making Anya uncomfortable, speaking as if she isn't here.

"Yes," Anya says. "I didn't know vampires existed before I met Xavier."

My mother sizes her up, unimpressed by her sexy, curvy form. Her type is the cold socialite. Too bad I don't like her type. "What do you do for a living, Anya?" Mom pauses. "Wait, you're a wet nurse aren't you?"

"So you feed strangers your...milk?" My father gestures in the air.

"Yes. I love my work," Anya says. "It brings me great joy to nourish people with my milk." She turns to me. "Of course, once we get married, my milk will only be for Xavier and our children."

Our children.

That most definitely makes my parents uncomfortable. They wanted a pureblood heir, not a mixed one. Too bad they can't always get what they want.

Mom and Dad blink, caught between disdain and incomprehension. "Are you...pregnant?" She shakes her head. "No, it's too early."

"I assure you, I plan to get her pregnant very soon. I'm not in the mood for any drama today, not when the most perfect woman said yes to me. I can't let my parents ruin our special day. "Haven't you always wanted a grandchild? We hope to give you the good news any day now. Anya will be the best mom any child could ask for."

Anya blinks, knowing I'm deliberately teasing them. The love between us makes our parents uncomfortable. Their own marriage was cold, and I'm so glad to have escaped that horrible fate.

"So, you're marrying her?" my father asks. There's a resigned expression on his face. He knows he can't stop fate.

"That's what I said." I keep my voice firm.

My mother leans back, nervously glancing at Anya. "She's going to require a lot of work. If she's going to make an entrance into society, she'll need lots of grooming and classes."

"Anya is perfect as she is. I don't want you turning her into one of those cold socialites you spend your time with. I love her as she is, and I have no plans to change her and mold her to your tastes. As you know, we're fated mates. She's the perfect match for me, the one destined to be by my side for life. I couldn't have asked for a better partner. She's the most caring, warm, and loving woman I've ever known, and her uniqueness makes her special." I lean forward, pressing a soft kiss on her lips. "So, I'm going to marry her whether you like it or not. You can either welcome her to the family with open arms and accept her as she is, or we can cut ties. The choice is yours."

"Xavier." Anya places her hand on my thigh, startled by the ultimatum.

"I won't stand for anyone judging and demeaning my wife. If I must cut my ties with you to preserve her happiness, it's what I'll do."

God knows I have enough money to move elsewhere and take care of her for life. I don't want my babygirl to be tainted by the ugliness in my family. As her husband, it's my duty to protect her loving nature.

My parents stare at each other, finally coming around. Turning to Anya, they say, "Welcome to the family, Anya."

CHAPTER 7
ANYA
SIX MONTHS LATER–

Our wedding takes place on a pleasant spring day. The venue is an ancient church decked with white flowers and finery, making it look like a page from a fairytale. Everything about the place is extravagant, from the satin cloth wrapped around the pews to the whole wall made of exquisite floor arrangements. The history of the church where Xavier's ancestors married shines through in the wooden, historical demeanor. Guests fill the hall, a wedding march by the orchestra being played as I walk down the aisle, the most radiant bride in existence. My groom's eyes are on me every step of the way, making me remember how desired I am.

My strapless wedding gown holds my milk jugs securely, the crystals studded in the bodice showing off my curves. My tits feel a little tender, but I know once we're done with the ceremony, my husband will take care of them. My wedding dress is a mermaid gown that clings to my curvy hips that Xavier was adamant I show off.

"I don't want you to hide behind your clothes, Anya," he

said when we picked out the dress. "I want to see your curvy, lush body in its natural form."

And so, I went with the figure-hugging gown that shimmers under the lights, showcasing my super pregnant belly. I know Xavier wanted to show that off to his family, letting them know that I am his mate who is carrying his seed.

With a shimmering tiara and veil, I look like a pregnant, curvy goddess in the custom-made designer wedding dress Xavier insisted I get. My six-month baby bump fills out the dress and I lovingly caress my swollen belly where our baby is growing, a proof of our union. When I found out I was pregnant just weeks after my first time with Xavier, we were both elated. Considering how often we'd been having sex, it didn't really come as a surprise, but when I realized that I was going to become a mom, I couldn't stop crying. Xavier held me close and whispered that he was happy to be a dad.

I gaze at the pews, noting Xavier's mom giving me a tight smile. I can see Francesca sitting behind her, her face curdled. I turn away, trying not to let my happy day be ruined by her.

Xavier's parents have accepted me into the family, especially after they found out that I was carrying their heir. After we announced my pregnancy, they softened up a little. Xavier's mom has been helping me with the strange feelings that come with bearing a vampire heir. As a human, I wasn't prepared for the level of energy it would take to carry Xavier's heir. I've been producing way more milk, and feeling fatigued, but my husband is always there for me, feeding me good food and taking care of my body. In the past few weeks, my face has been splashed all over the papers, the news of Xavier's marriage captivating the nation. He's a famous billionaire, after all, and I'm coming to realize what an important role I'll be playing as his wife.

However, as come to stand facing Xavier, all my reservations melt away. After he proposed to me, he insisted that I move in with him. We annulled my wet nurse contract, and I quit my job at the agency to be my vampire husband's full-time milkmaid. Our life ever since has been joyful. I was okay with a small wedding, but Xavier went all out, insisting that I deserved the best.

"I want to show you off to everyone, babygirl," he said, caressing my stomach. "Imagine how good you'll look pregnant with my baby in that wedding dress. The whole world will know you're mine, that your vampire Daddy bred you well and good."

And so, we decided to have a grand ceremony with all his friends and family in attendance. Since I'm an orphan, most of the people who attended from my side were friends. I ignore the camera shutters going off everywhere as I gaze up at my husband through my veil. Dressed in a white suit that matches my dress, he is all my dreams come true. The media is here to cover our special day, something that I still need to get used to. But for my husband, I'm ready to do anything.

"You're beautiful." He mouths, his striking green gaze trailing over my pregnant body, latching onto my swollen stomach. He kisses my bare stomach every night, saying how much he loves my womanly, pregnant body. I never thought I could have that with anyone.

"Do you take Anya Saunders to be your lawfully wedded wife..." The priest's voice echoes behind us, but we only have eyes for each other. I know Xavier loves me and I love him. I feel like the most beautiful woman on earth because this sexy, caring man loves me. The way he gazes at me, full of lust and admiration, takes my breath away every time. My heart is so happy because he looks healthy. I've been feeding my milk every day, enjoying our sexy milking sessions more and more as my pregnancy progresses and my body becomes more sensitive to his touch. Feeding him fills a need deep inside me, and I want him to know I'll always be there for him.

"Yes, I do." My vampire Daddy's mouth parts, and I can't help but stare at his sexy lips. I want them on mine, kissing me, and making me feel like the most precious woman alive. I take another step closer to him. The wedding rehearsals have been exhausting, especially in my state, but I'm so happy we get to have this fairytale wedding. It's all I've ever wanted.

The priest turns to me, repeating the same question. I only have eyes for Xavier. His hot body encased in a fitted suit makes my pussy flutter. I can't wait to start a family with him.

"Yes, I do." My words echo in the church as more camera flashes go off.

The priest finishes up, and then, the words I've been waiting to hear leave his mouth. I don't miss Xavier's mom wiping away a tear, realizing that she must be happy because her son found love. Despite her reservations, Xavier's mom knows that we're really in love.

"You may now kiss the bride."

Xavier is on me in a heartbeat, snaking his big Daddy arms around my waist and pulling my pregnant body close. Our lips meet in a heated explosion, the passion between us unmistakable.

I feel good on the inside, knowing Francesca is watching us like this, me pregnant with Xavier's child, kissing him, and becoming his wife. I want the whole world to know that I am his.

The kiss drags on until we're both hot and needy, craving each other.

When the priest clears his throat, I pull away, staring into my husband's beautiful face.

"I love you," he says. "At last, you're mine."

"I'm yours," I admit, leaning close to him as the media takes pictures of us as Mr. And Mrs. Tallon.

CHAPTER 8
XAVIER

My gorgeous bride stands before me, her milky melons leaking behind her magnificent white wedding dress. At last, the wedding is over and I've got Anya all to myself.

"Welcome home, Mrs. Tallon." Standing by her side in our bedroom, I kiss her cheek, my hands holding her pregnant stomach and caressing it through the gown. She looks like a wet dream in that wedding gown, and I can't wait to take it off her.

"I can't believe we're finally married." She gazes at the bed where we've made love for months. "This is our bedroom..."

"Tallon Manor is now your home," I whisper in her ear, kissing her jaw and ear. As my fingers move over her swollen belly, I notice that she leans into me, sinking into my embrace. "You're now the lady of the manor and my wife. And soon, you'll be a mom."

"Mmm...About that," She turns around, and her big stomach bumps into my hard erection tenting my trousers. Her fingers grab the lapel of my coat and push it off my shoulders. She hungrily begins to pop the buttons of my shirt, sexual need evident in her gestures. "I've been horny all morning, Daddy. I need to feel your cock inside me."

Ever since Anya got pregnant, she's been needing more sex, and I'm only too happy to spoil my fertile, milky wife. My shirt comes off, and falls on the floor, leaving my chest naked for my wife. She runs her hand all over my rippling muscles, placing her palm where my heart beats. Leaning forward, she presses a kiss between my ribs, her soft mouth making my cock even harder.

My fingers immediately reach for the zipper at the back of her gown and drag it down to part the dress. When the air brushes her bare back, she cuddles against me. I push the gown off her, and it pools on the floor, revealing my wife's massive milkers that are all engorged with cream, and her big stomach that is the stuff of my breeding fantasies.

"God, you're so fucking hot, Anya." I trail my lips down her shoulders, cupping and kissing her tits. Milk begins to leak from her tips, streaking all over her swollen belly. She's a fertile, milky goddess, all knocked up with her Daddy's seed. I kiss her big belly, running my hands all over its surface. She moans as her pussy clenches, dripping for me. Anya loves it when I shower attention on her pregnant belly. "Daddy loves your pregnant body so much." I kiss her belly button, rubbing my stubble over her smooth, round stomach. "You're so beautiful when you're swollen with Daddy's seed and filled with milk." I shower more love on her womb that's nourishing my heir inside it. There's no part of her that I'm not completely in love with. My lips trail down, pulling off her panties and finding her shaven mound. When I press a kiss on it, her legs buckle. More milk drips from her teats and collects at her seam. I lick her pussy, tasting the cream and honey there. "Look how wet you get when you're horny." I hold her up, knowing she needs to lie down. I kiss her thighs, all the way to her feet. "I love every inch of your body, babygirl. You're Daddy's perfect milkmaid." When my lips meet her toes, I can feel them curl.

"Daddy…Please…" Her entire body is shivering, burning with the need for my cock.

I stand up, knowing it's time to claim my wife. Coming up to her height, I seize her lips in a passionate kiss. Anya melts into me, opening her mouth and letting me thrust my tongue inside to taste her innocence. She'll always be the woman who changed my life and showed me what love and caring look like. "You're mine now, baby."

I push her back, laying her down softly on the bed. Then, I proceed to strip until I'm as naked as her. There's no hiding my heavy organ that throbs between my legs, needing to be inside my wife's snug little pussy.

"Open your legs, babygirl. Let Daddy see the pussy he bred so well."

With a groan, Anya opens her legs, and my balls tighten at the sight of her glistening, pink pussy, all wet and ready to be ravished by her Daddy. I climb on top of her, positioning my cock at her entrance. With one smooth glide, I fill her up, sliding between those puffy pink pussy lips and claiming Anya's womb.

"Aaahhh…" she cries out as her silky walls are stretched. Her pussy is so tight, fitting snugly around my dick as I revel in the feeling of being sheathed in my wife's heat. There's no place I was to be except inside her, giving her pleasure.

My hands cover her stomach, my mouth coming down on one engorged tit. I massage her baby bump as I begin to move inside her in slow, shallow thrusts. "Mmm...I love the way your pregnant stomach bounces, babygirl. Daddy wants to keep you bred with his babies forever."

Anya smiles, loving that idea. Her fingers reach for me, needing to feel me close.

"Rest on my tits, Daddy. They're so tender and achy for your mouth." She pushes her hands under her fat udders and holds them up. The puffy tips wet with cream make my throat go dry.

Without hesitation, I put my mouth on one leaking, achy teat and suck a mouthful of cream. She cries louder when the letdown hits, her walls squeezing my dick in response.

"Mmm..baby, Daddy loves it when you do that." My fangs dig into her teats and her cries intensify. I pull and tug on her teat, pulling more milk from her nourishing mounds, suckling on that squishy nipple. My cock continues moving inside her, a deep need building in my balls. Watching her milky, pregnant form write under me, knowing I knocked her up, makes me so hot I already want to come inside her.

I pull my dick out almost all the way and thrust back in as I suction harder.

"Oh...." Anya's fat tits bounce, spraying milk into my mouth. They are extra-sensitive because of the pregnancy and she feels everything more intensely. I fuck her deeper this time, grinding my cock into her fleshy channel and hitting her womb. "Daddy....yes...you make me feel so good."

I drill her cunt ruthlessly with hard, deep strokes, my fat cock squelching in and out of my wife's wet pussy. All the while, I hold her pregnant belly and drink her nourishing nectar. Almost done with one tit, I extract my fangs, licking over her aroused nipple. "Who do you belong to, babygirl? Who owns this perfect body?"

"You, Daddy," she cries, as I pound into her sweet little cunt ruthlessly.

"I'm going to make you come now, Mrs. Tallon, and fill you up with my seed. Are you ready, baby?" My cock hits her sweet spot, making her see stars. When she screams, her cunt contracting around my cock, I know she's coming.

"Daddy!" Her sweet voice fills my ears as an orgasm sweeps over her body. My hips continue thrusting rhythmically into her hot hole. Her fleshy walls massage me, and I come inside her, my mouth on those lush titties. My lips wrap around her other tit, licking her teat like a cat. Milk explodes in my mouth as I orgasm inside my wife, filling her up with my baby-making seed. If she wasn't pregnant already, she'd be now.

Waves of ecstasy drown me as Anya and I come together as man and wife. Her pussy grips me hard, milking me for my seed, and I give it to her, filling her to the brim until my seed is trickling down her thigh. She's mine now, fully claimed as my fertile wife. The orgasm sparks through my cells, as we become one in a blaze of heated passion. Life feels perfect when I'm inside my pregnant wife, loving her body, and drinking her nourishing liquid that makes me feel powerful and alive. With her, my life is complete.

When the orgasm fades, I'm still kissing my wife's milky boobs, my fangs draining her creamy liquid. I pull my dick out of her, loving the way my seed trickles down her pussy.

"That was amazing," she says. "Like always. I'm such a lucky girl because my husband always takes care of me."

"I'm the lucky one," I say, kissing her half-drained tip. "I get to call you my wife, and enjoy this lush, curvy body every day."

Anya sits up, her bare back resting against the cushioned headboard. I lay my head on her stomach, her ripe, heavy breasts leaning over my mouth. I suckle them gently as she caresses my hair, enjoying a quiet moment after our orgasm.

"I love you," she says, her fingers threading through my hair. She presses a kiss to my temple, feeding me her nipple. I suckle cream from it, enjoying her sweet, reviving taste. "Being a vampire's milkmaid was the best decision I made in life."

I smile around her teat, lapping up her cream with wet, greedy sounds.

"Me too, babygirl." I rest on her pregnant stomach, feeling ecstatic because I'm finally with my mate and the woman who has healed me and brought me back to life. "You've exceeded all my expectations and brought me back to life with your love and care. There's nowhere I want to be except here, lying on this stomach that I bred, tasting your sweet cream. You're my forever, Anya. I love you."

With this loving woman by my side, I know I'll have a life filled with happiness and laughter.

About the Author

Jade Swallow is an author of super steamy novels. She loves reading and writing filthy tales featuring all kinds of kinks. Follow her on Instagram @authorjadeswallow for news about upcoming books.

Sign up for my newsletter here to get updates about my upcoming releases: subscribepage.io/eiSMM1

ALSO BY JADE SWALLOW

Looking for more paranormal and omegaverse erotica by me? Check out these books:

Stranded on the Shifter's Mountain: A Fated Mates Werewolf Shifter Romance with Breeding and Pregnancy

A Hucow Nanny for the Alpha Daddies: An age gap reverse harem fated mates omegaverse novella with pregnancy and milking (Omegaverse Daddies #1)

Alpha Daddy's Omega: An age gap pregnancy knotting and pregnant short story with arranged marriage (Omegaverse Daddies #2)

The Sea God's Fertile Bride : An age gap tentacle monster erotica (Married and Pregnant Monster Shorts #1)

Beauty and the Orc: An age gap orc daddy monster romance (Married and Pregnant Monster Shorts #2)

The Dragon's Maid : Age gap fated mates dragon monster romance with pregnancy, knotting, and milking (Married ad Pregnant Monster Shorts #4)

Love Daddy kink, breeding, and milking? Check out these books:

Breeding the Babysitter: A forbidden age gap billionaire romance with pregnancy (Forbidden Daddies #1)

Mountain Daddy's Curvy Maid : A grumpy-sunshine age gap romance with pregnancy and lactation (Mountain Daddies #1)

Pregnant by the Mafia Boss : A forbidden age gap mafia romance with pregnancy (Mafia Daddies #1)

Claiming my Ex's Dad: A forbidden age gap erotica

Milked by my Best Friend's Mom : An age gap lesbian erotic novella

Short story bundles:

Summer Heat Series Bundle (Summer Heat #1-5)

Feeding Fantasies Box Set (Feeding Fantasies 1-5 + 2 bonus shorts)

Creamy and Pregnant Short Stories (Billionaires & Hucows #1-5)

Love dark college romances with steam and plot? Check out this one:

Broken (Twisted Souls #1)

She's a serial killer on a mission, and he's her next target. But things get complicated when she begins falling for him...

www.ingramcontent.com/pod-product-compliance
Ingram Content Group UK Ltd.
Pitfield, Milton Keynes, MK11 3LW, UK
UKHW021416060325
4886UKWH00020B/192

9 798339 565086